Merlin
The Magical Puppy

MERLIN AND THE BIG TOP

KEITH LITTLER

CARLTON
BOOKS

Merlin the puppy was playing at the harbour with his friends Kizzie and Charlotte. Charlotte was very excited because she was going to the circus the next day.

"Wow!" Merlin barked. "Can I come?"

Charlotte explained that no pets were allowed.

"But that's not fair," Merlin sighed. "I'd love to go to the circus."

Merlin went back to his kennel feeling very miserable, but then he had an idea. He could use his magic collar.

So he closed his eyes and concentrated very hard. "I want to go to the circus. In fact, I want to be the star of the circus."

He opened his eyes hopefully, but nothing had changed.

Merlin was sure that his collar must be broken. "Oh, I wish I could be the star of the circus," he sighed.

As soon as Merlin said the magic word, "wish", his collar began to glow and sparkle.

Suddenly he appeared in a circus ring under a colourful big top.

As Mr Pickles, the ringmaster, introduced him, Merlin climbed up to the trapeze.

There was a gasp of amazement from the crowd and everyone looked up.

"You will be sure to catch me, won't you?" Merlin barked across to Oscar from his platform high above the ground.

"Don't worry," Oscar purred. "You can rely on me."

On the second swing Merlin let go of his trapeze. But Oscar did not catch him.

"Oops! Silly me," Oscar purred. "I seem to have missed."

Poor Merlin fell to the ground with a thump, landing right between Ernie and Miss Parkway.

"Are you OK, Merlin?" Ernie asked.

"Just a bit dizzy," Merlin barked weakly.

The crowd was not very impressed. Mr Pickles hurriedly made a dramatic announcement.

"Ladies and gentlemen, Merlin the Magical Puppy will now dive off the high tower into a tub of water."

The crowd gasped once again and the drums rolled.

At the top of the tower, Merlin counted to three and then he jumped. There was a very loud clang! Naughty Oscar had not filled the tub with water.

Poor Merlin!

The crowd booed and hissed.

Mr Pickles took Merlin and Oscar back to the dressing room. "We need something that will excite our audience," he boomed.

"I know," Merlin barked, "but things keep going wrong. And now I've got a bad ear and a bad nose!"

"I have a great idea," Oscar purred. "Something dramatic. We can shoot Merlin from a cannon."

"What do you mean?" Mr Pickles asked.

"It's simple. We place Merlin in a cannon, light a fuse and then, boom, we shoot him into a safety net. The crowd will love it."

Mr Pickles was impressed. "What do you think, Merlin?"

"I'm not sure about the 'boom' bit," Merlin whined.

"You'll be fine," Oscar purred. "Trust me."

Mr Pickles returned to the ring and made his big announcement.

"You will be careful to use the short fuse, won't you?" Merlin asked Oscar nervously from inside the cannon.

"Don't you worry about a thing," Oscar tittered. "I am sure this will go with a bang."

Then Oscar took one of the special long fuses from a box and lit it.

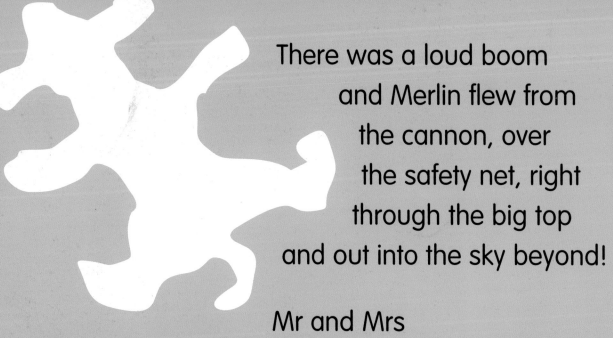

There was a loud boom
and Merlin flew from
the cannon, over
the safety net, right
through the big top
and out into the sky beyond!

Mr and Mrs
Crabtree, with their niece Charlotte,
watched in amazement.

"That has to be a world record,"
Mr Crabtree said.

Half a mile away, Reg the Hedge was taking a walk when he heard a rustle in the bushes. He looked up and there was Merlin's tail sticking out.

"Hello, Merlin. What are you doing there?"

"Oooh, I've got a leaf up my nose," Merlin snorted. "I wish I'd never joined the circus!"

As soon as he said the magic word, "wish", his collar began to glow and sparkle.

Suddenly Merlin was back home.

Charlotte was really pleased to see him. "Great news, Merlin! You can come to the circus with us tomorrow."

Merlin sighed. "Oh, that's all right," he barked. "I think I've had enough of the circus for one day, thank you."